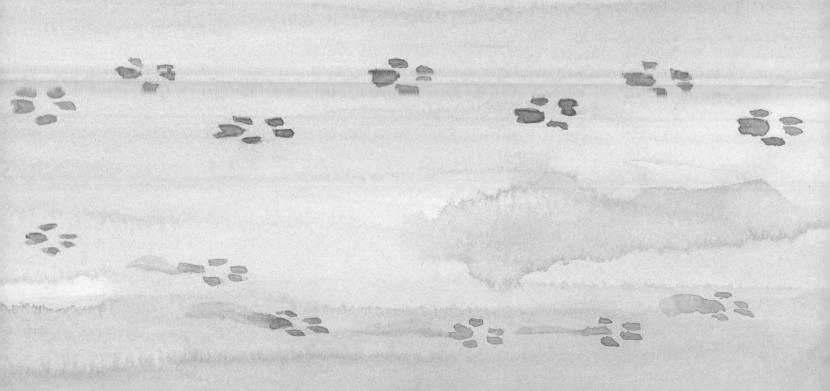

What Are You Doing, Benny?

Words by **CARY FAGAN**

Pictures by **KADY MACDONALD DENTON**

tundra

Tundra Books, an imprint of Penguin Random House Canada Young Readers, a Penguin Random House Company

Library and Archives Canada Cataloguing in Publication

Fagan, Cary, author
    What are you doing, Benny? / Cary Fagan ; Kady MacDonald Denton, illustrator.

Issued in print and electronic formats.
ISBN 978-1-77049-857-0 (hardcover). — ISBN 978-1-77049-859-4 (EPUB)

    I. Denton, Kady MacDonald, illustrator II. Title.

PS8561.A375W43 2019   jC813'.54   C2017-902906-1
                                                C2017-902907-X

Published simultaneously in the United States of America by Tundra Books of Northern New York, an imprint of Penguin Random House Canada Young Readers, a Penguin Random House Company

Library of Congress Control Number: 2017940265

Edited by Tara Walker
The artwork in this book was rendered in ink, watercolor and gouache on 140 lb. Arches Hotpress.
The text was set in Garamouche.

Printed and bound in China

www.penguinrandomhouse.ca

1   2   3   4   5   22   21   20   19   18

For Emilio — C.F.

For S.W. — K.M.D.

Benny?

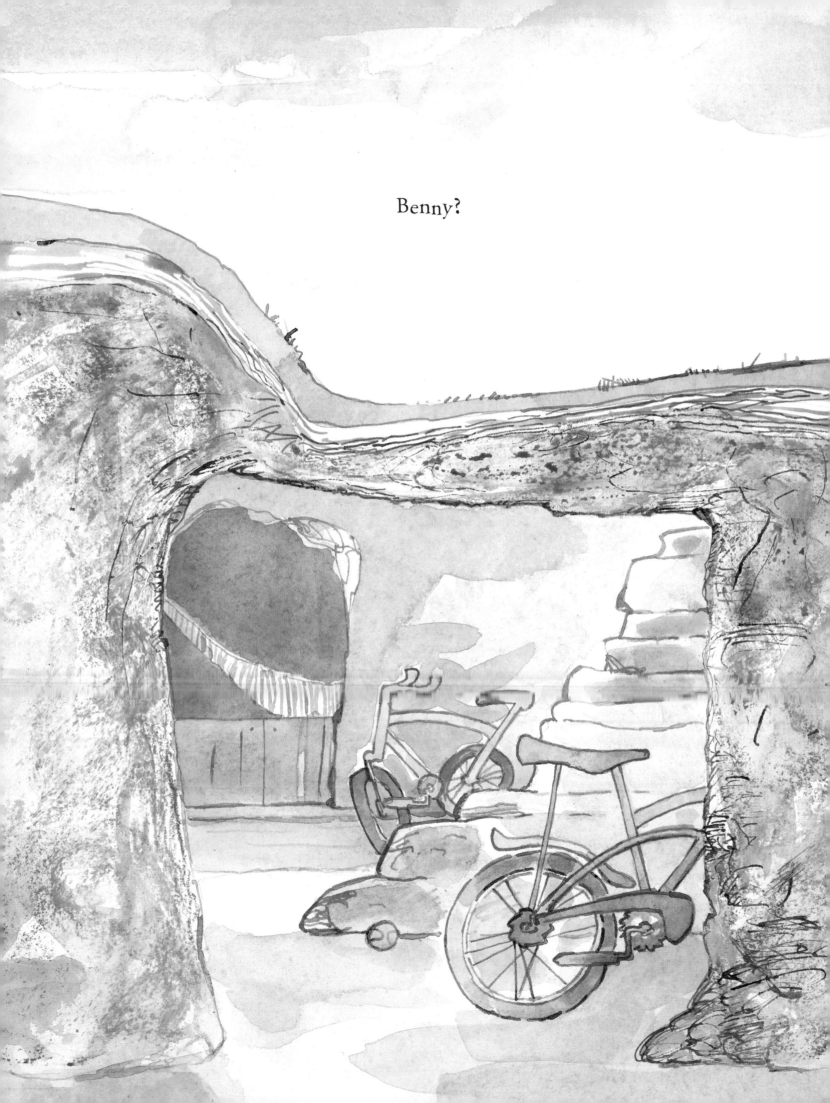

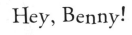

Hey, Benny!

What are you doing, Benny? Building a fort?

Neat!

I'm really good at building forts.

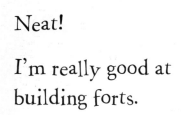

So can I help, Benny?

No, said Benny.

Benny?

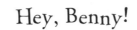

Hey, Benny!

What are you doing, Benny? Making a potion?

I'm terrific at making potions.

I like to mix relish and maple syrup and tomato juice and hot sauce. But you know what the secret is?

Mashed banana.

So can I help,
Benny?

No, said Benny.

Benny?

Hey, Benny!

What are you doing, Benny?
Making a paper airplane?

I'm a genius at making paper airplanes. I have a special way of bending the wings up at the tips.

It makes them soar and swoop and then land perfectly.

So can I help, Benny?

No, said Benny.

I sighed really loud.

Then I went to my own room.

I took out my box of puppets.

Benny appeared in the doorway. He looked at me.

I'm going outside, he said.

Benny walked away.

I followed him outside.

Benny?

Hey, Benny!

What are you doing, Benny?
Riding your bike?

I bet you don't think I can keep up.

But you should see how fast I can go
on my two-wheeler now. Zoom!

So can I ride with you, Benny?

No, said Benny.

Benny?

Hey, Benny!

What are you doing, Benny?
Petting the neighbor's cat?

She really likes me.

It's because I have a special way of
scratching her just behind the ears.

So can I pet the cat too, Benny?

No, said Benny.

Benny?

Hey, Benny!

What are you doing, Benny?

Lying on the grass and looking up at the sky?
That's one of my favourite things to do.

I like how the grass tickles and the way a
cloud sometimes looks like a boot or a cow.

So can I lie on the grass with you, Benny?

No, said Benny.

I sighed again and went back into the house.

I laid each puppet on my bed.

Then I set up the puppet stage.

Benny appeared in the doorway.
He looked at me.

I'm going to the kitchen, he said.

Benny walked away.

I followed him to the kitchen.

Benny?

Hey, Benny!

What are you doing, Benny? Making a sandwich?

I like the way you use mustard and sliced chicken and mayonnaise and pickles. In fact, you make the best sandwiches in the world. I'm hungry, too.

So can I have a sandwich, Benny?

No, said Benny.

Benny?

Hey, Benny!

What are you doing, Benny? Playing your guitar?

I'm really good at making up songs.

I'll make up a song right now.

I have a brother
and his name
is Benny.

When he makes
a joke it's
really funny.

And I would
give him
all my money.

So will you play your guitar while I sing, Benny?

No, said Benny.

This time I didn't sigh.
I just went back to my room.

I put a puppet on one hand
and a puppet on the other hand.

Do you want to play with me?

No.

No, no, no!

Benny appeared in the doorway.
He looked at me.

Want to watch me shoot hoops?
he asked.

No, thanks,
I said.

Want to watch me paint my model car?

You know what, Benny?
I said. It's kind of boring
just to watch.

I started the puppet show again.

Benny went away.

After a while, Benny came back.
He looked at me.

He held out a plate.

Benny? Hey, Benny?

Who's that sandwich for?
For **ME**? No fooling?

Thanks, Benny!

I ate the sandwich.

It was delicious.

We could put on a puppet show together.

We could make it really funny and then really scary and then really silly.

So do you want to put on a puppet show with me, Benny?

Yes, said Benny.

Yes?

Yes.